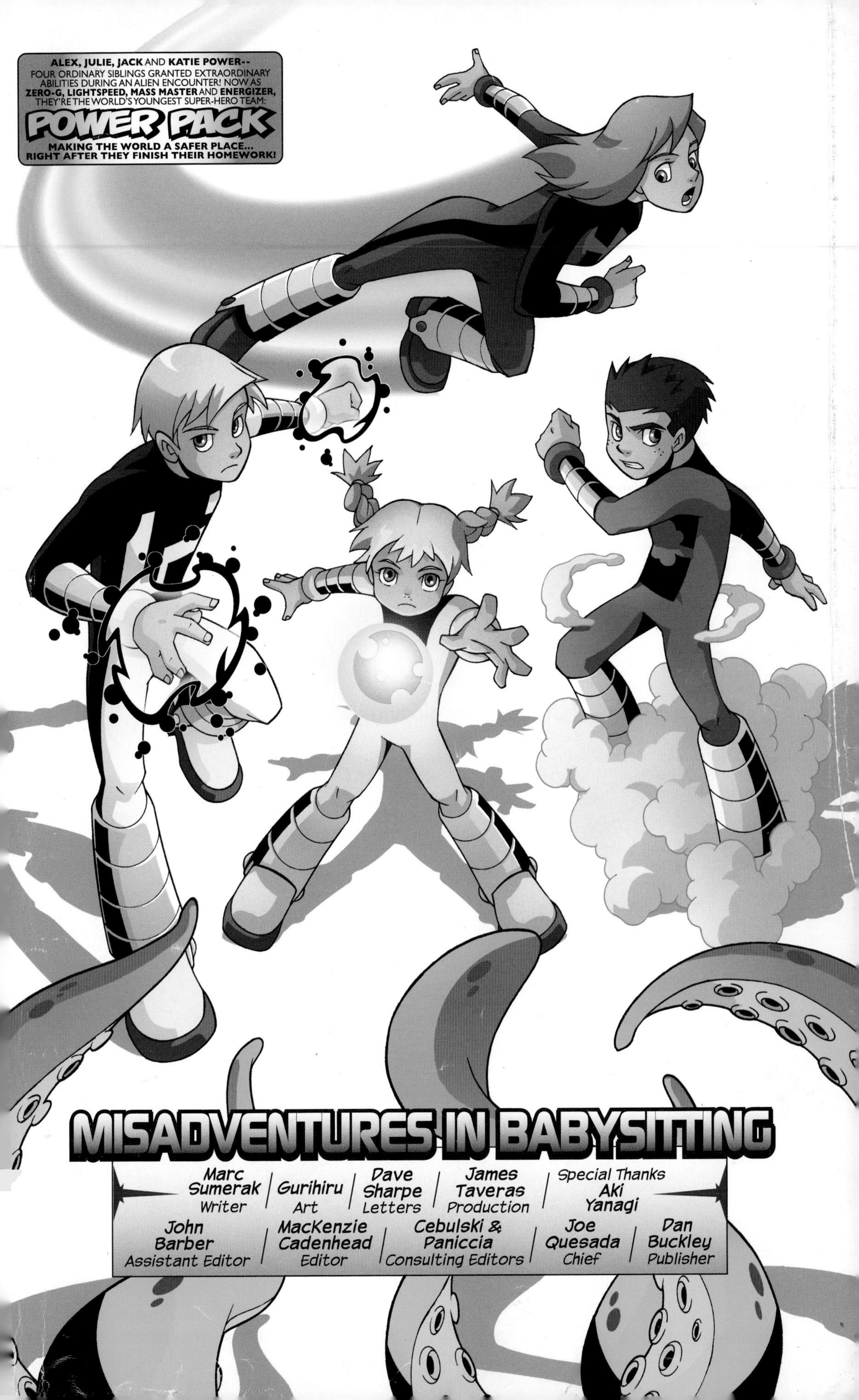
ALEX, JULIE, JACK AND KATIE POWER--
FOUR ORDINARY SIBLINGS GRANTED EXTRAORDINARY ABILITIES DURING AN ALIEN ENCOUNTER! NOW AS ZERO-G, LIGHTSPEED, MASS MASTER AND ENERGIZER, THEY'RE THE WORLD'S YOUNGEST SUPER-HERO TEAM:
POWER PACK
MAKING THE WORLD A SAFER PLACE... RIGHT AFTER THEY FINISH THEIR HOMEWORK!
MISADVENTURES IN BABYSITTING
Marc Sumerak Writer
Gurihiru Art
Dave Sharpe Letters
James Taveras Production
Special Thanks Aki Yanagi
John Barber Assistant Editor
MacKenzie Cadenhead Editor
Cebulski & Paniccia Consulting Editors
Joe Quesada Chief
Dan Buckley Publisher

VISIT US AT

www.abdopub.com

Spotlight, a division of ABDO Publishing Company Inc., is the school and library distributor of the Marvel Entertainment books.

Library bound edition © 2006

Library of Congress Cataloging-in-Publication Data

Misadventures in Babysitting

ISBN 1-59961-034-5 (Reinforced Library Bound Edition)

All Spotlight books are reinforced library binding
and manufactured in the United States of America

Spotlight

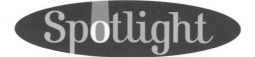

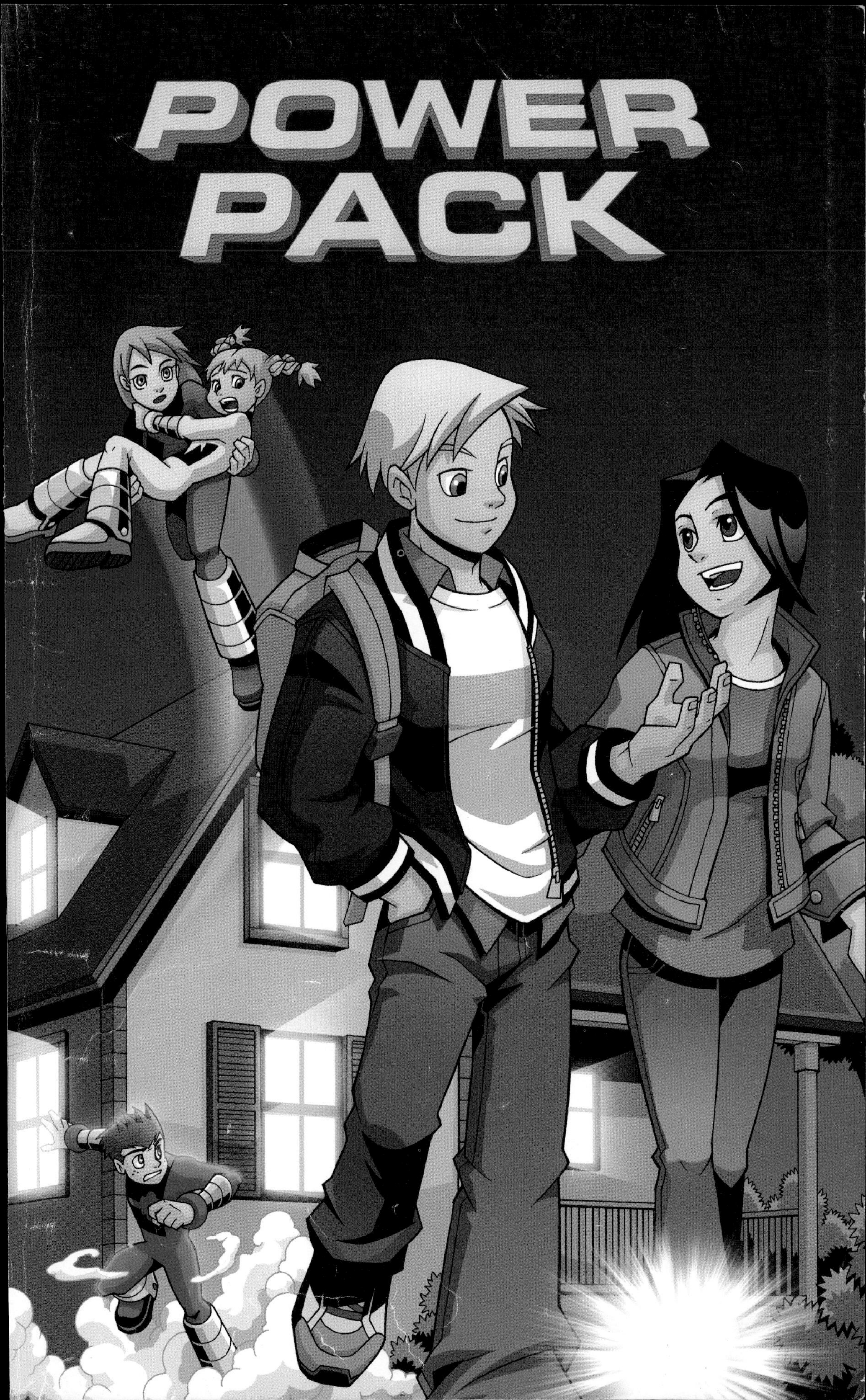
POWER PACK

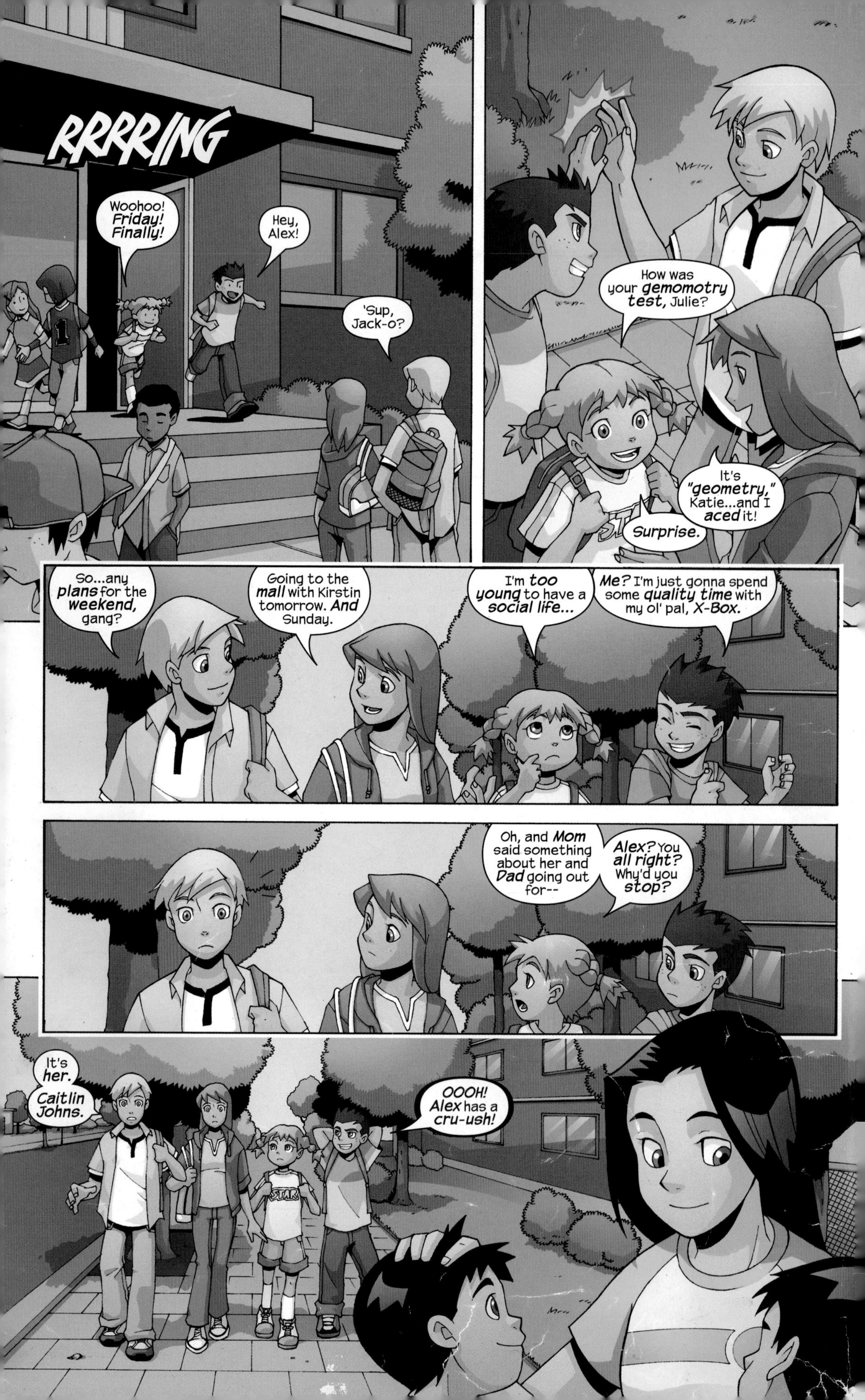
RRRRING
Woohoo! Friday! Finally!
Hey, Alex!
'Sup, Jack-o?
How was your gemomotry test, Julie?
It's "geometry," Katie...and I aced it!
Surprise.
So...any plans for the weekend, gang?
Going to the mall with Kirstin tomorrow. And Sunday.
I'm too young to have a social life...
Me? I'm just gonna spend some quality time with my ol' pal, X-Box.
Oh, and Mom said something about her and Dad going out for--
Alex? You all right? Why'd you stop?
It's her. Caitlin Johns.
OOOH! Alex has a cru-ush!

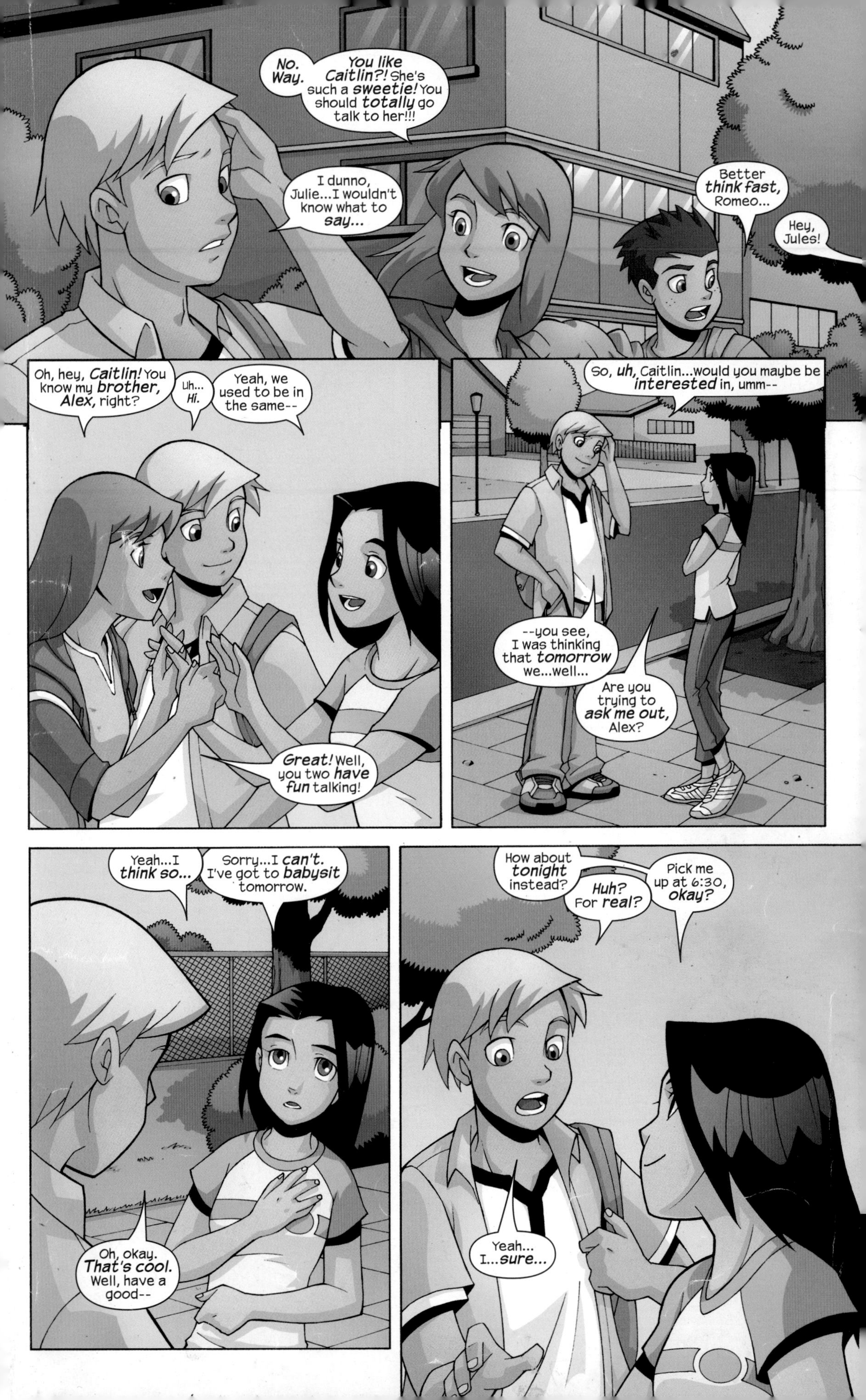
No. Way.
You like Caitlin?! She's such a sweetie! You should totally go talk to her!!!
I dunno, Julie...I wouldn't know what to say...
Better think fast, Romeo...
Hey, Jules!
Oh, hey, Caitlin! You know my brother, Alex, right?
Uh... Hi.
Yeah, we used to be in the same--
Great! Well, you two have fun talking!
So, uh, Caitlin...would you maybe be interested in, umm--
--you see, I was thinking that tomorrow we...well...
Are you trying to ask me out, Alex?
Yeah...I think so...
Sorry...I can't. I've got to babysit tomorrow.
Oh, okay. That's cool. Well, have a good--
How about tonight instead?
Huh? For real?
Pick me up at 6:30, okay?
Yeah... I...sure...

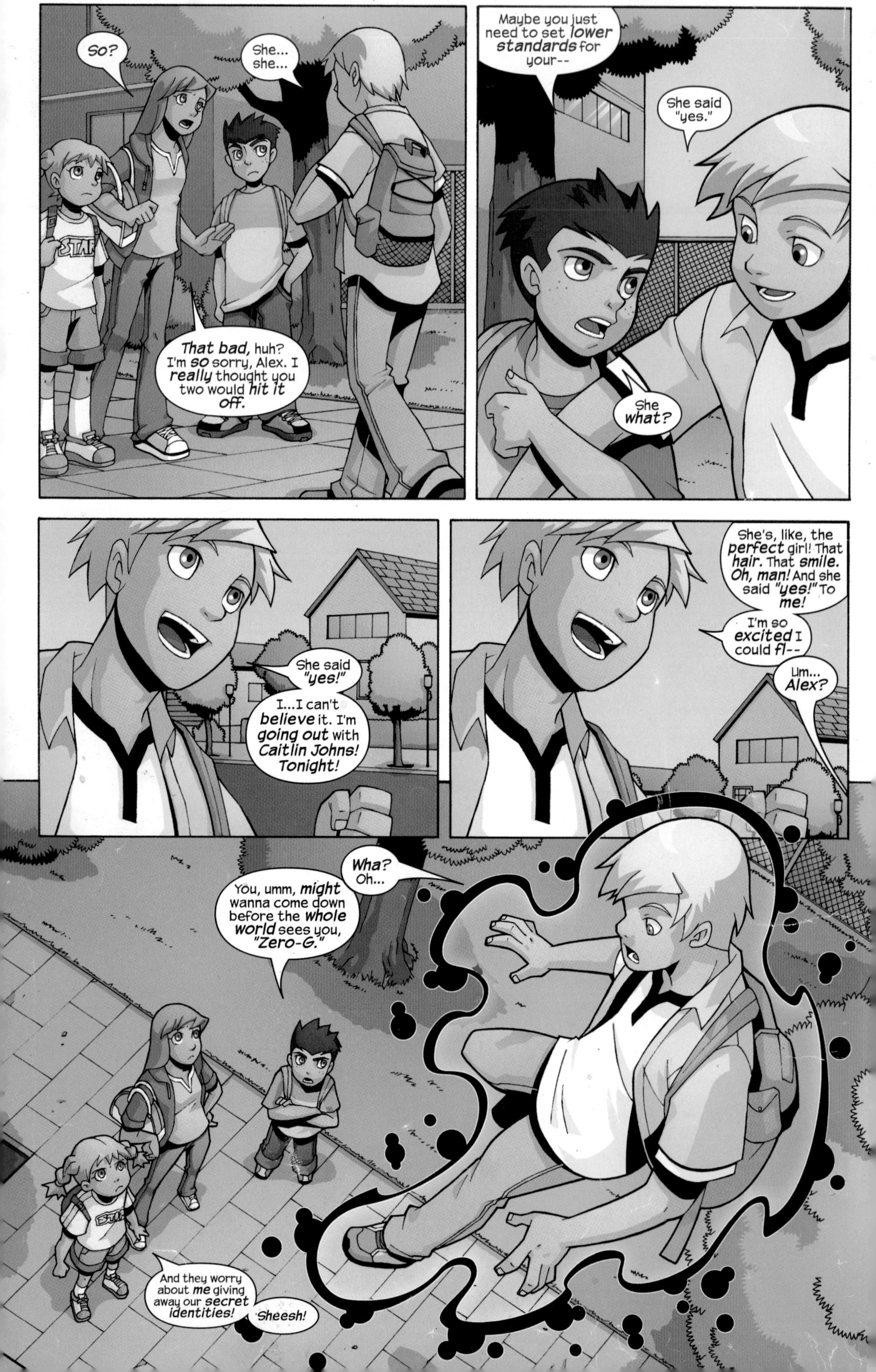
So?
She... she...
That bad, huh? I'm so sorry, Alex. I really thought you two would hit it off.
Maybe you just need to set lower standards for your--
She said "yes."
She what?
She said "yes!"
I...I can't believe it. I'm going out with Caitlin Johns! Tonight!
She's, like, the perfect girl! That hair. That smile. Oh, man! And she said "yes!" To me!
I'm so excited I could fl--
Um... Alex?
Wha? Oh...
You, umm, might wanna come down before the whole world sees you, "Zero-G."
And they worry about me giving away our secret identities!
Sheesh!

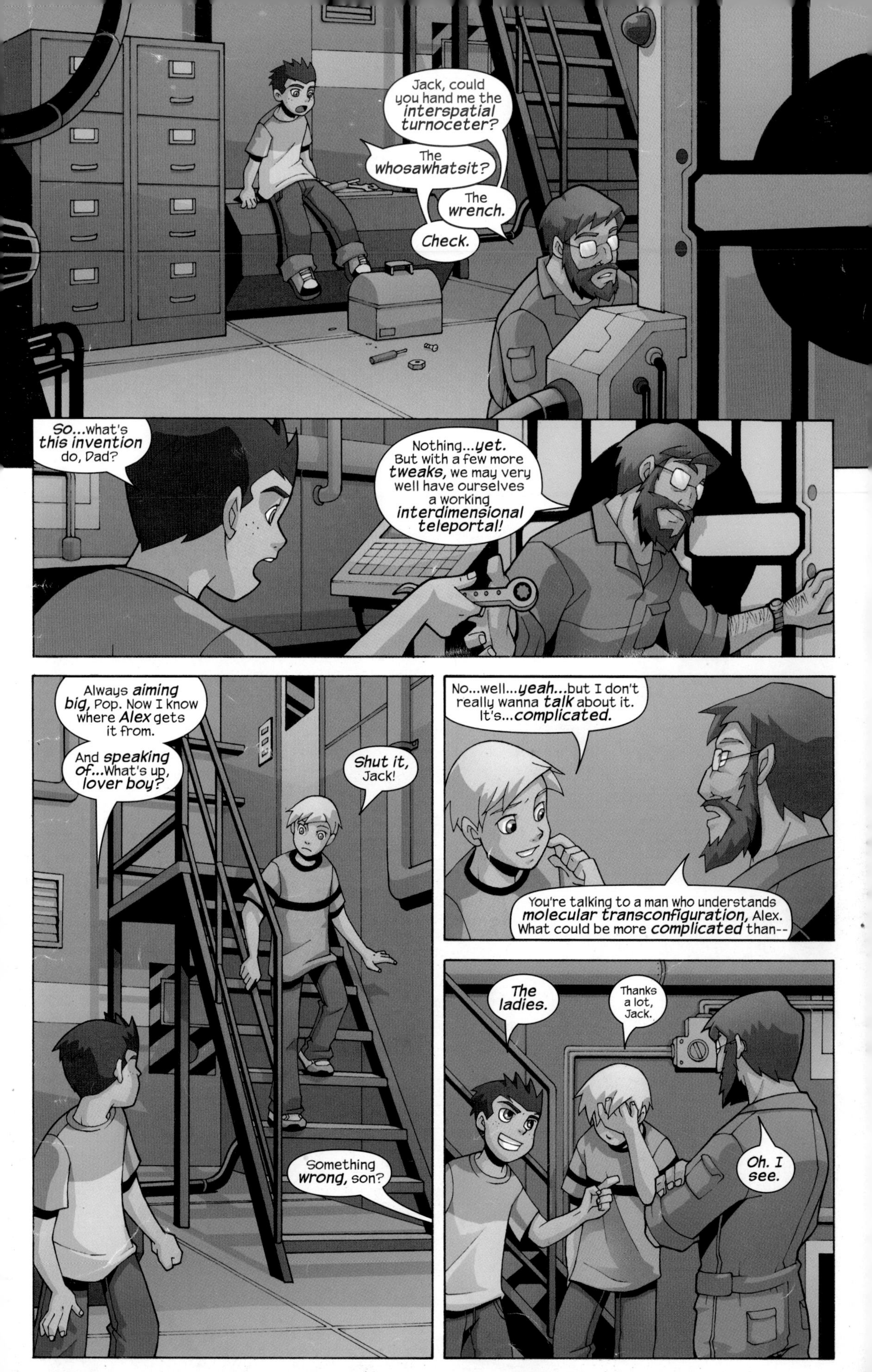
Jack, could you hand me the interspatial turnoceter?
The whosawhatsit?
The wrench.
Check.
So...what's this invention do, Dad?
Nothing...yet. But with a few more tweaks, we may very well have ourselves a working interdimensional teleportal!
Always aiming big, Pop. Now I know where Alex gets it from.
And speaking of...What's up, lover boy?
Shut it, Jack!
Something wrong, son?
No...well...yeah...but I don't really wanna talk about it. It's...complicated.
You're talking to a man who understands molecular transconfiguration, Alex. What could be more complicated than--
The ladies.
Thanks a lot, Jack.
Oh. I see.

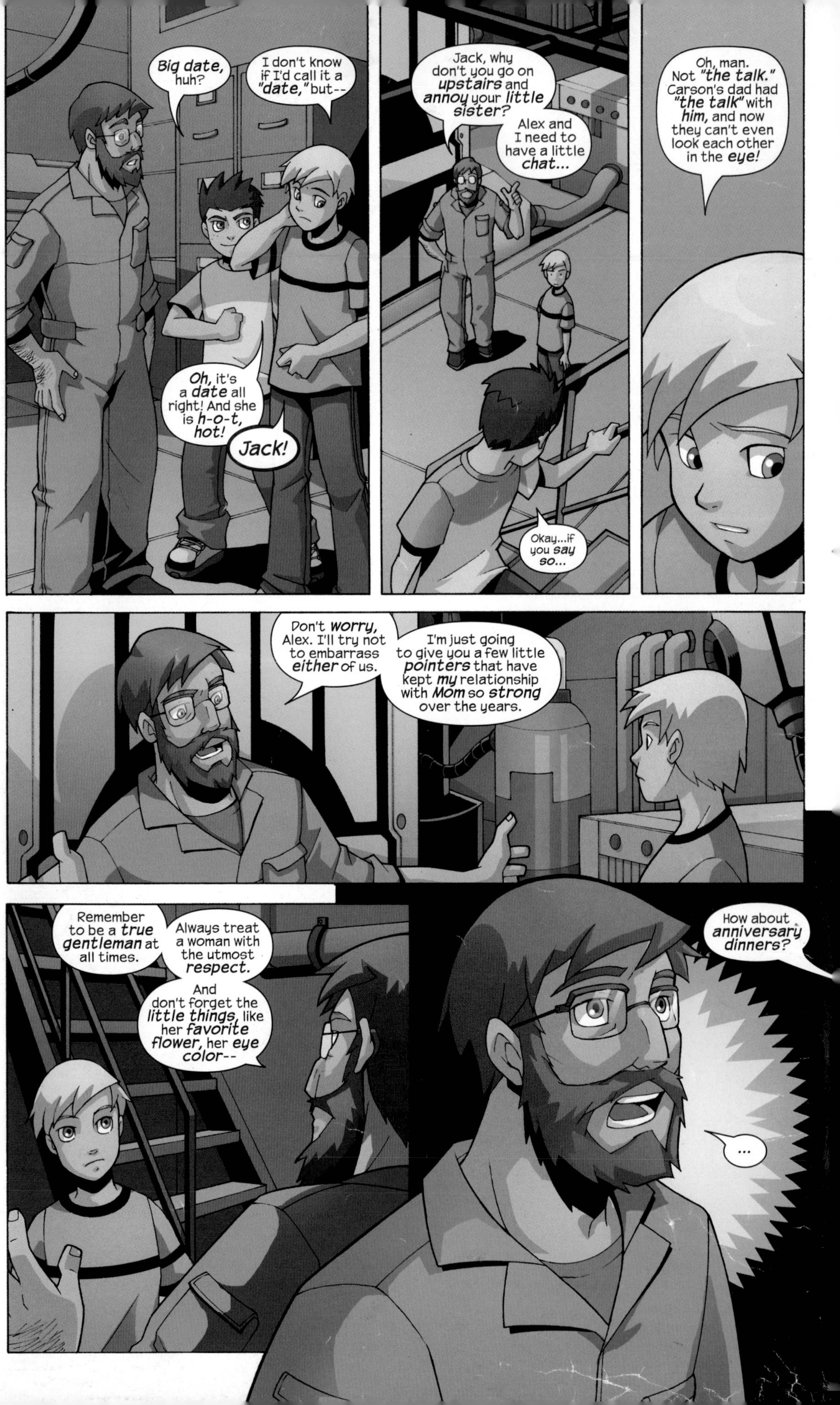
Big date, huh?
I don't know if I'd call it a "date," but--
Oh, it's a date all right! And she is h-o-t, hot!
Jack!
Jack, why don't you go on upstairs and annoy your little sister?
Alex and I need to have a little chat...
Okay...if you say so...
Oh, man. Not "the talk." Carson's dad had "the talk" with him, and now they can't even look each other in the eye!
Don't worry, Alex. I'll try not to embarrass either of us.
I'm just going to give you a few little pointers that have kept my relationship with Mom so strong over the years.
Remember to be a true gentleman at all times.
Always treat a woman with the utmost respect.
And don't forget the little things, like her favorite flower, her eye color--
How about anniversary dinners?
...

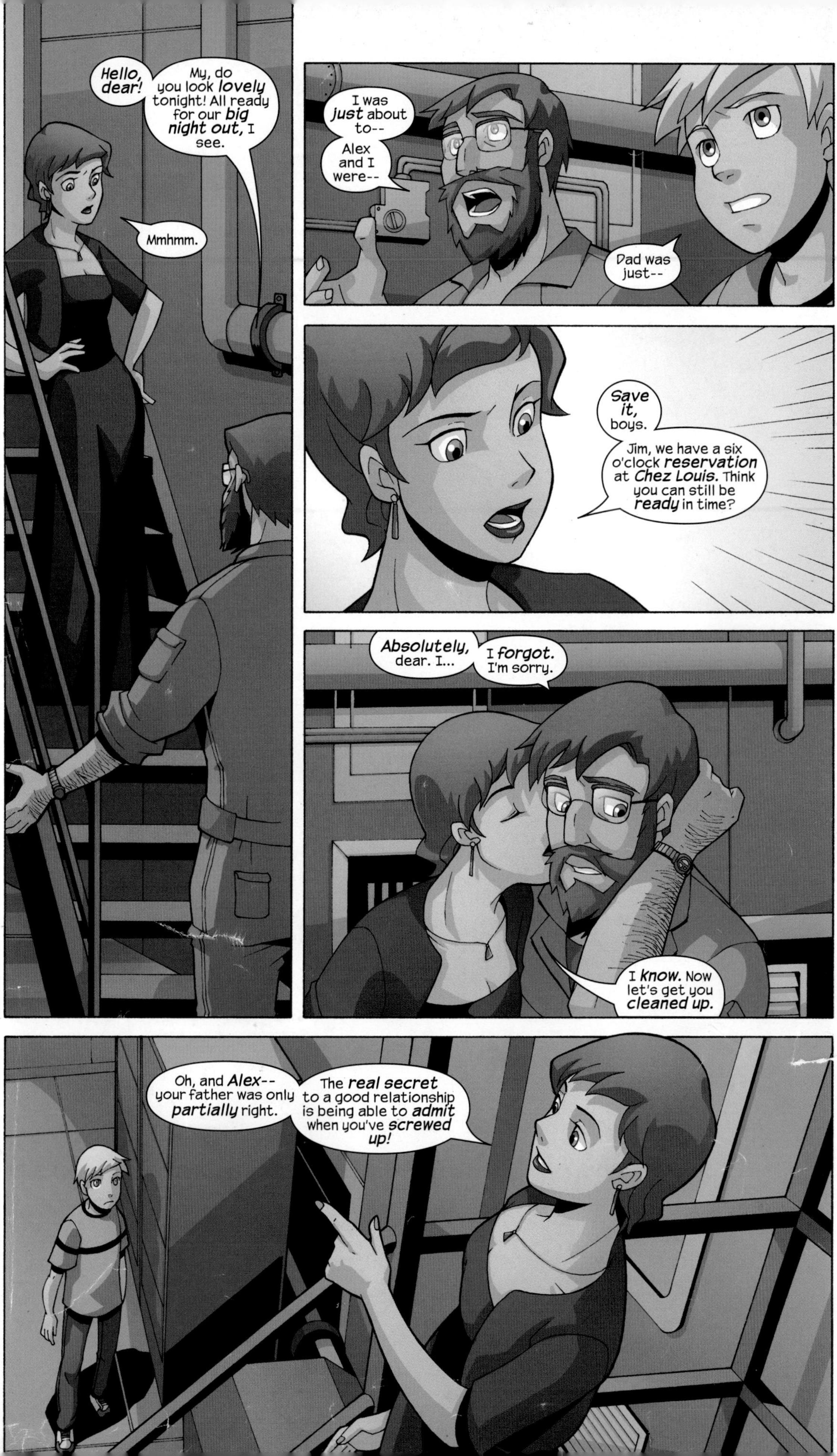
Hello, dear!
My, do you look lovely tonight! All ready for our big night out, I see.
Mmhmm.
I was just about to--
Alex and I were--
Dad was just--
Save it, boys.
Jim, we have a six o'clock reservation at Chez Louis. Think you can still be ready in time?
Absolutely, dear. I...
I forgot. I'm sorry.
I know. Now let's get you cleaned up.
Oh, and Alex-- your father was only partially right.
The real secret to a good relationship is being able to admit when you've screwed up!

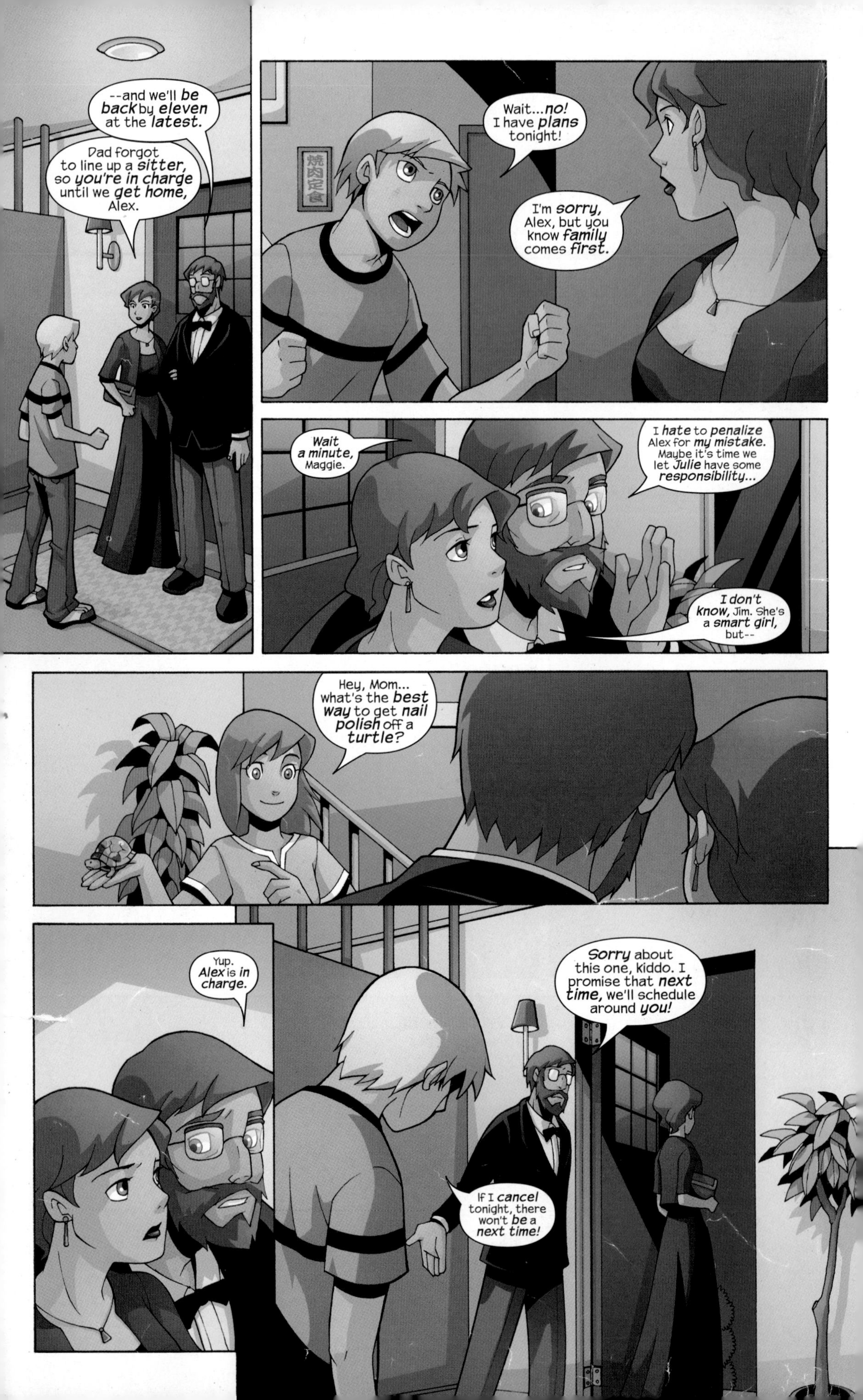
--and we'll be back by eleven at the latest.
Dad forgot to line up a sitter, so you're in charge until we get home, Alex.
Wait...no! I have plans tonight!
I'm sorry, Alex, but you know family comes first.
Wait a minute, Maggie.
I hate to penalize Alex for my mistake. Maybe it's time we let Julie have some responsibility...
I don't know, Jim. She's a smart girl, but--
Hey, Mom... what's the best way to get nail polish off a turtle?
Yup. Alex is in charge.
Sorry about this one, kiddo. I promise that next time, we'll schedule around you!
If I cancel tonight, there won't be a next time!

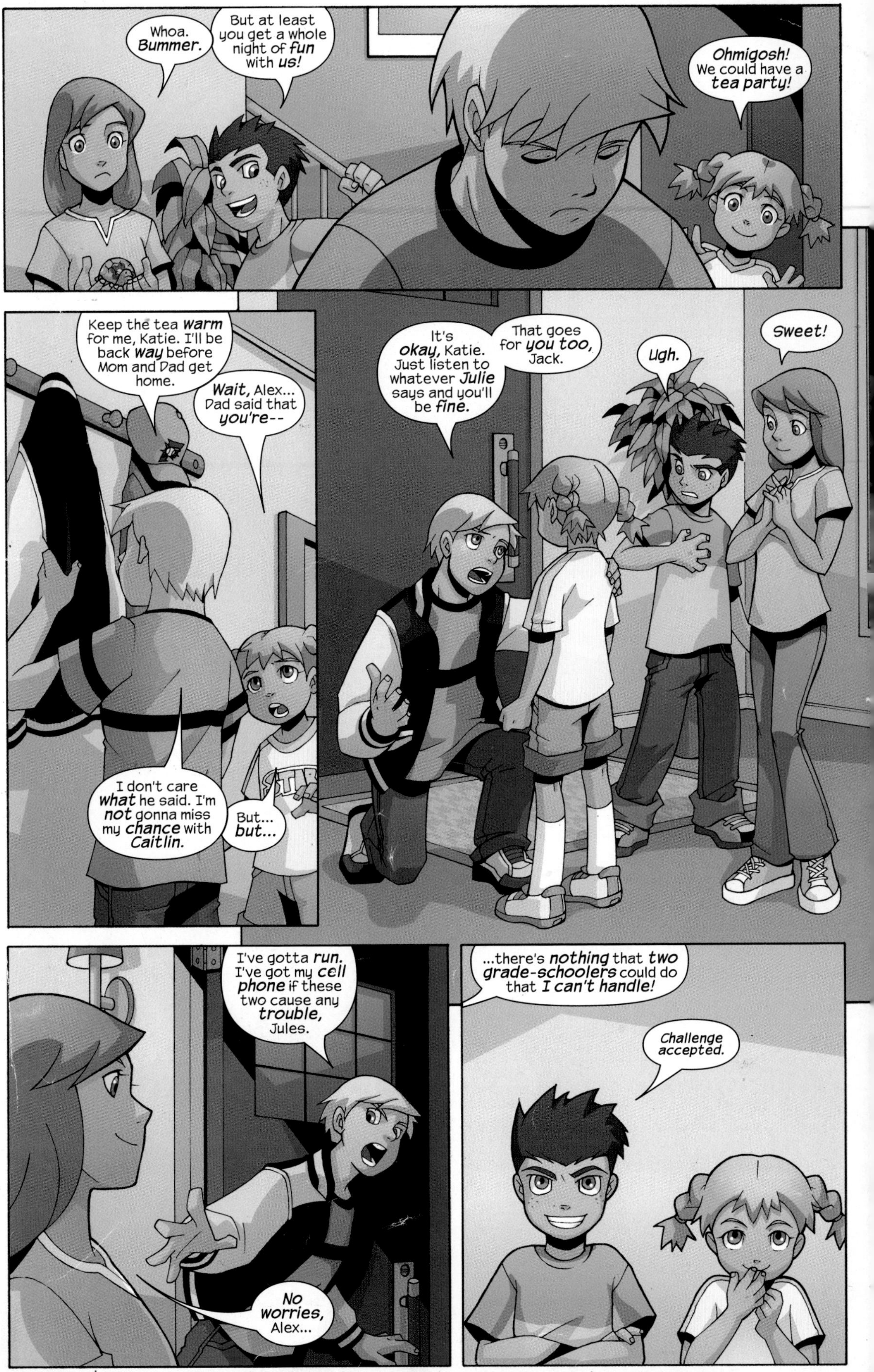

Whoa. Bummer.
But at least you get a whole night of fun with us!
Ohmigosh! We could have a tea party!
Keep the tea warm for me, Katie. I'll be back way before Mom and Dad get home.
Wait, Alex... Dad said that you're--
I don't care what he said. I'm not gonna miss my chance with Caitlin.
But... but...
It's okay, Katie. Just listen to whatever Julie says and you'll be fine.
That goes for you too, Jack.
Ugh.
Sweet!
I've gotta run. I've got my cell phone if these two cause any trouble, Jules.
No worries, Alex...
...there's nothing that two grade-schoolers could do that I can't handle!
Challenge accepted.

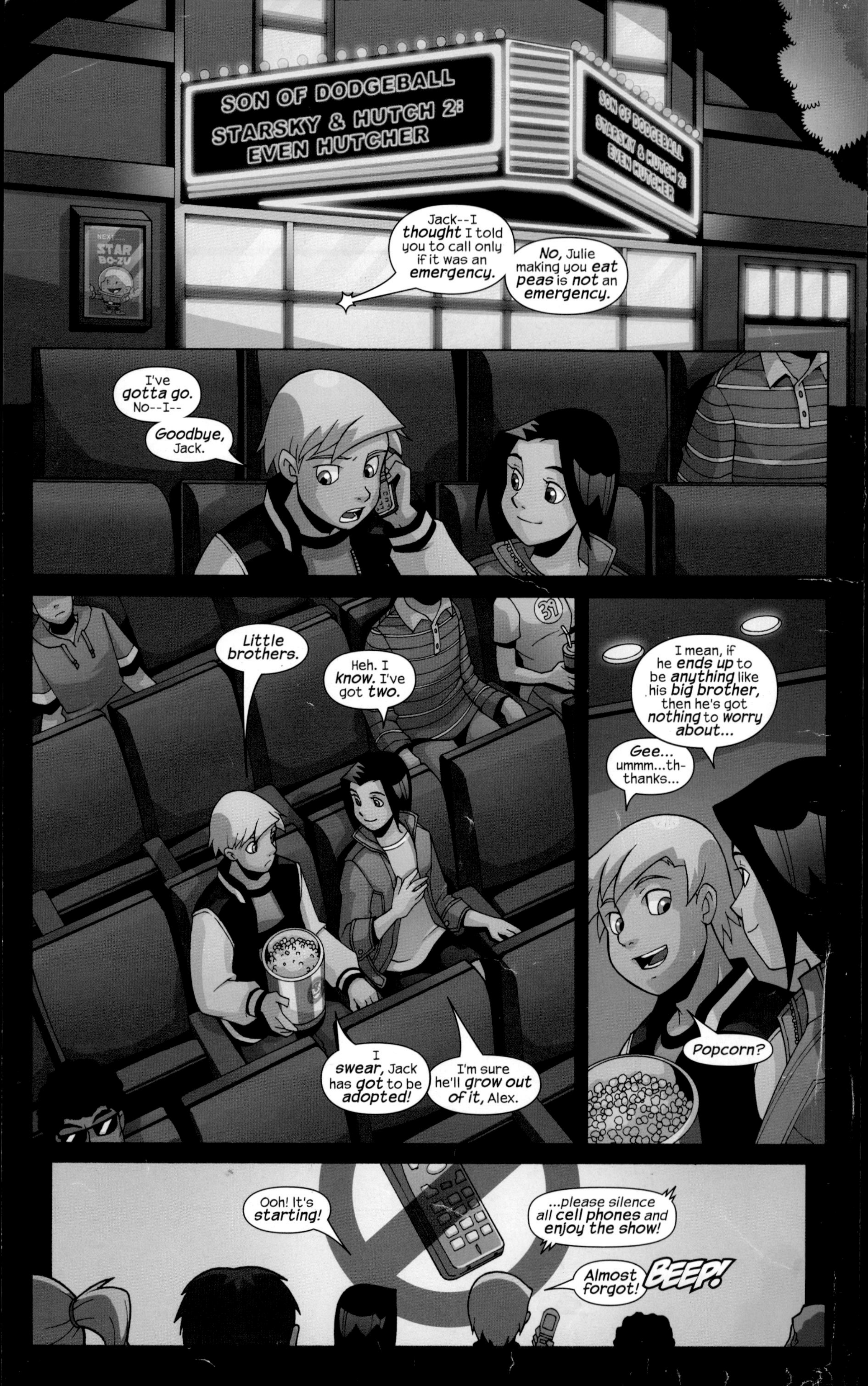
SON OF DODGEBALL
STARSKY & HUTCH 2: EVEN HUTCHER
NEXT... STAR BO-ZU
Jack--I thought I told you to call only if it was an emergency.
No, Julie making you eat peas is not an emergency.
I've gotta go. No--I--
Goodbye, Jack.
Little brothers.
Heh. I know. I've got two.
I swear, Jack has got to be adopted!
I'm sure he'll grow out of it, Alex.
I mean, if he ends up to be anything like his big brother, then he's got nothing to worry about...
Gee... ummm...th-thanks...
Popcorn?
Ooh! It's starting!
...please silence all cell phones and enjoy the show!
Almost forgot!
BEEP!

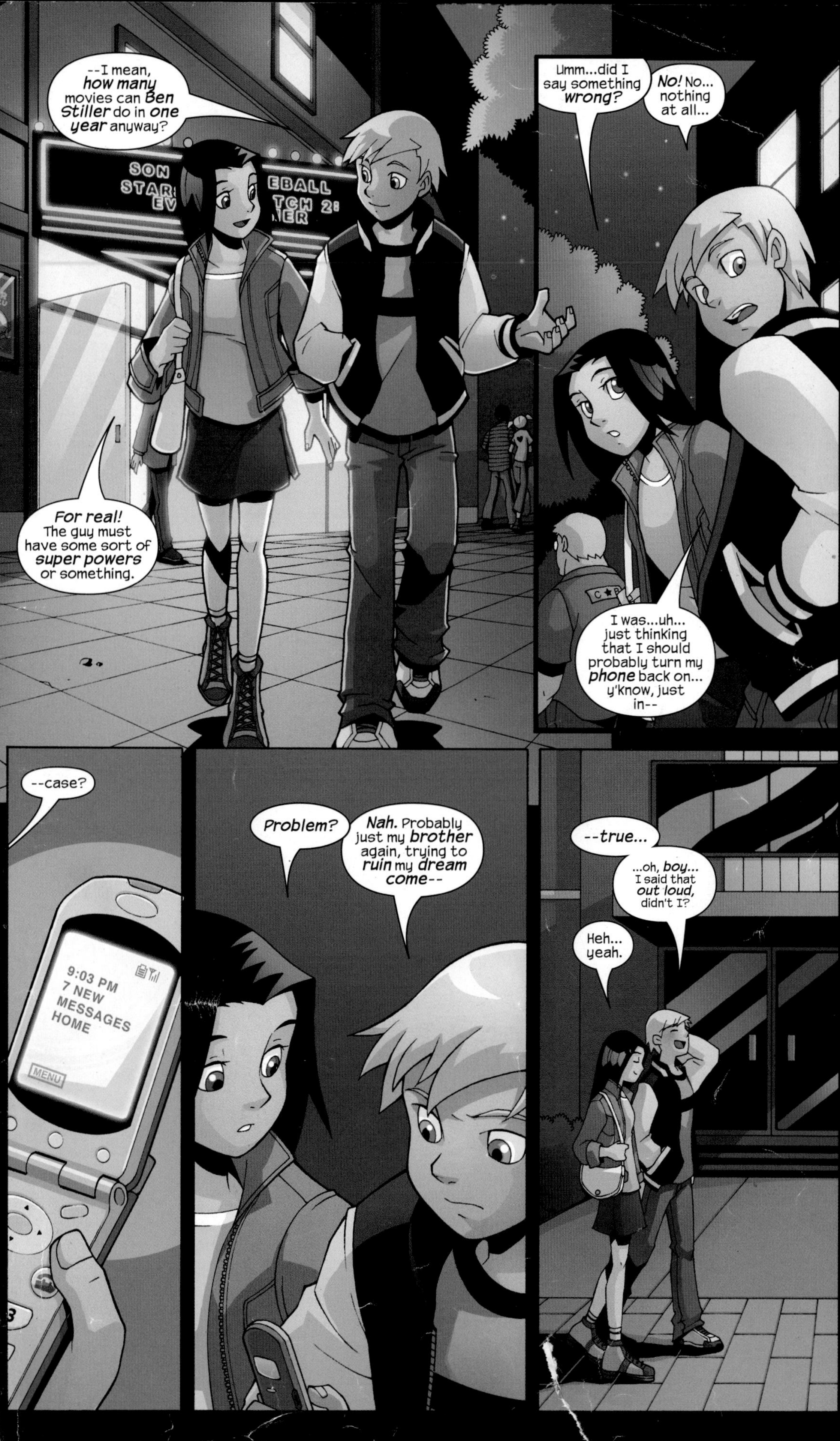
--I mean, *how many* movies can *Ben Stiller* do in *one year* anyway?
For real! The guy must have some sort of *super powers* or something.
Umm...did I say something *wrong?*
No! No... nothing at all...
I was...uh... just thinking that I should probably turn my *phone* back on... y'know, just in--
--case?
9:03 PM
7 NEW MESSAGES
HOME
MENU
Problem?
Nah. Probably just my *brother* again, trying to *ruin* my *dream come*--
--*true*...
...oh, *boy*... I said that *out loud,* didn't I?
Heh... yeah.

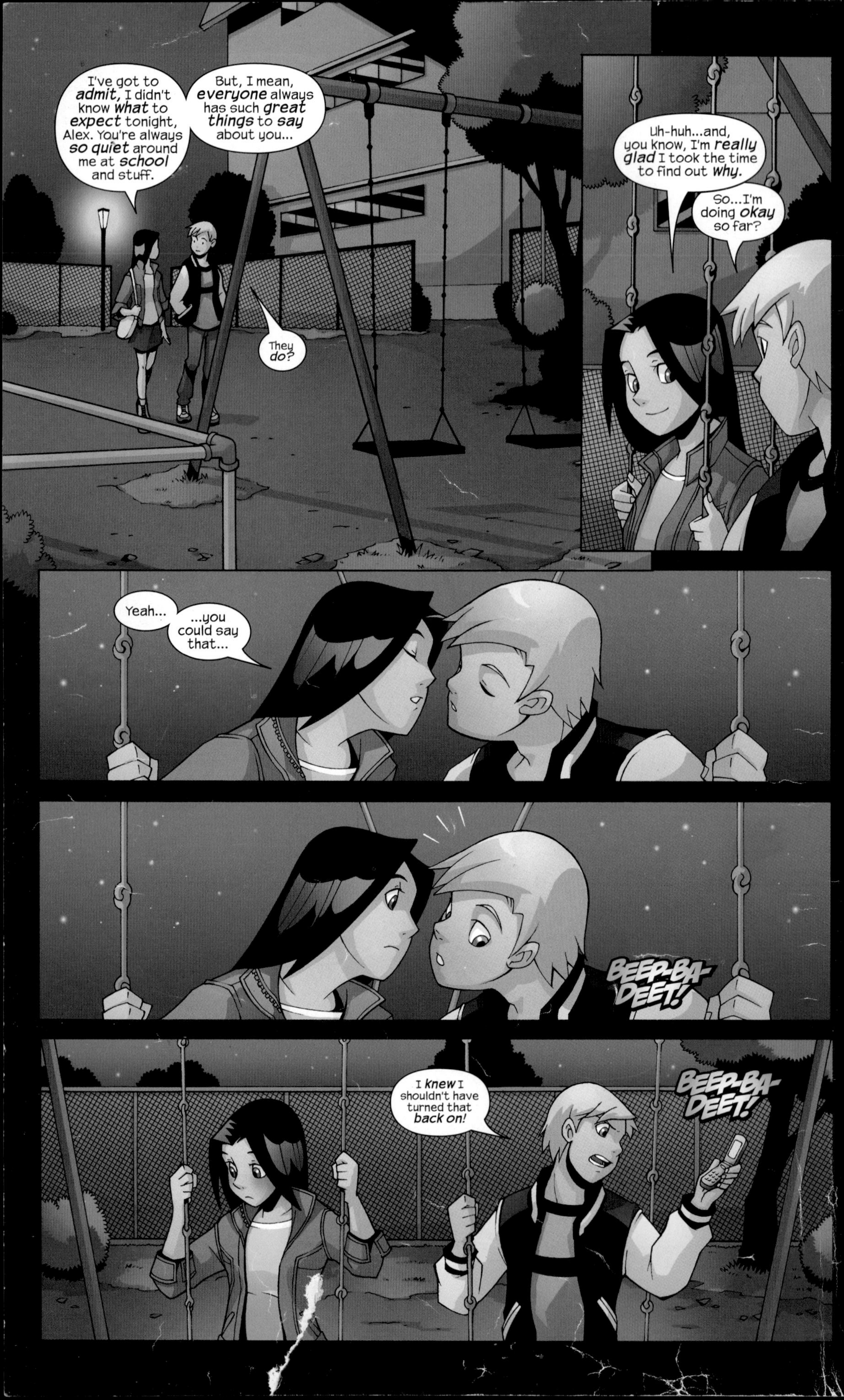
I've got to admit, I didn't know what to expect tonight, Alex. You're always so quiet around me at school and stuff.
But, I mean, everyone always has such great things to say about you...
They do?
Uh-huh...and, you know, I'm really glad I took the time to find out why.
So...I'm doing okay so far?
Yeah...
...you could say that...
BEEP-BA-DEET!
BEEP-BA-DEET!
I knew I shouldn't have turned that back on!

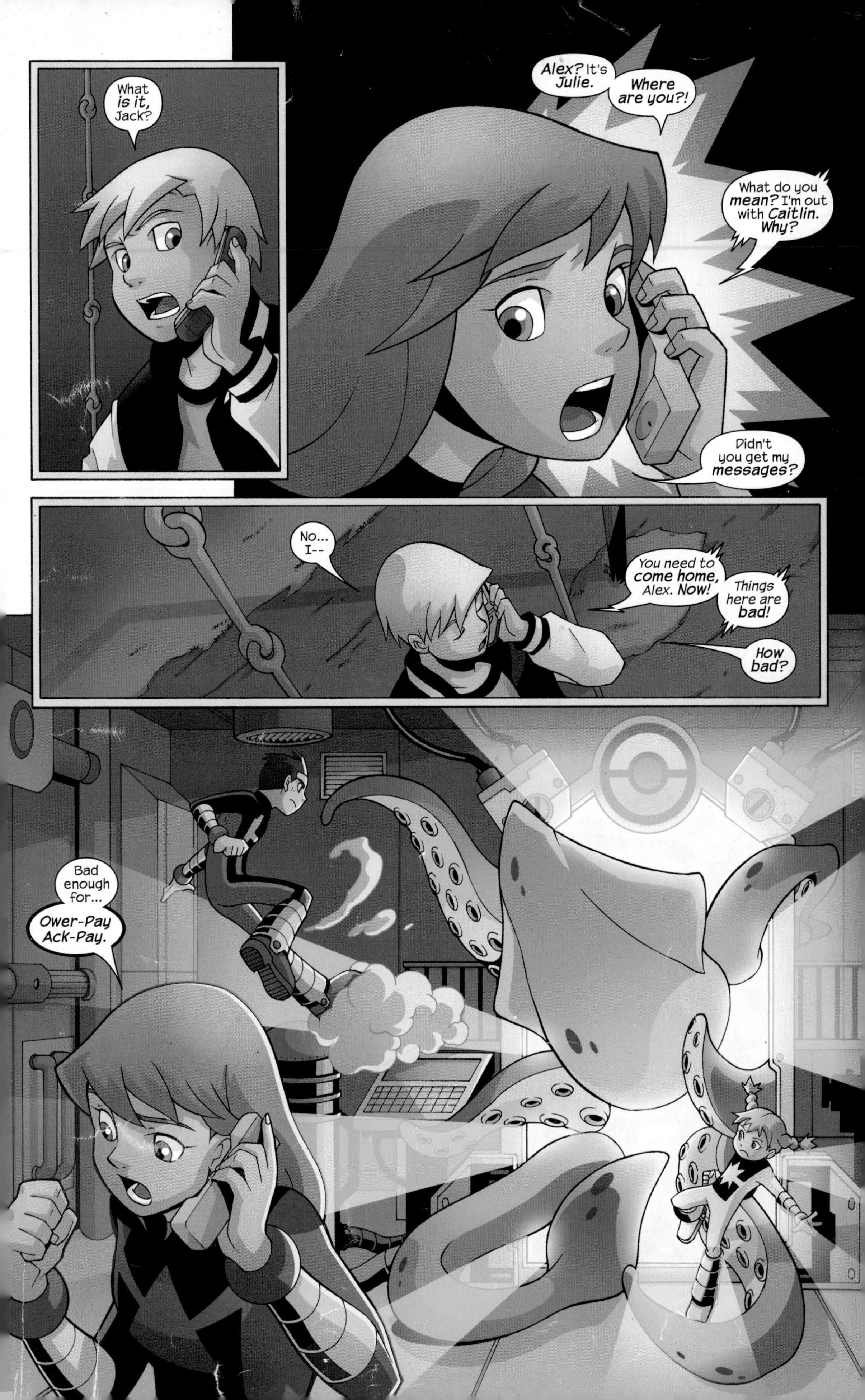
What is it, Jack?
Alex? It's Julie.
Where are you?!
What do you mean? I'm out with Caitlin. Why?
Didn't you get my messages?
No... I--
You need to come home, Alex. Now!
Things here are bad!
How bad?
Bad enough for...
Ower-Pay Ack-Pay.

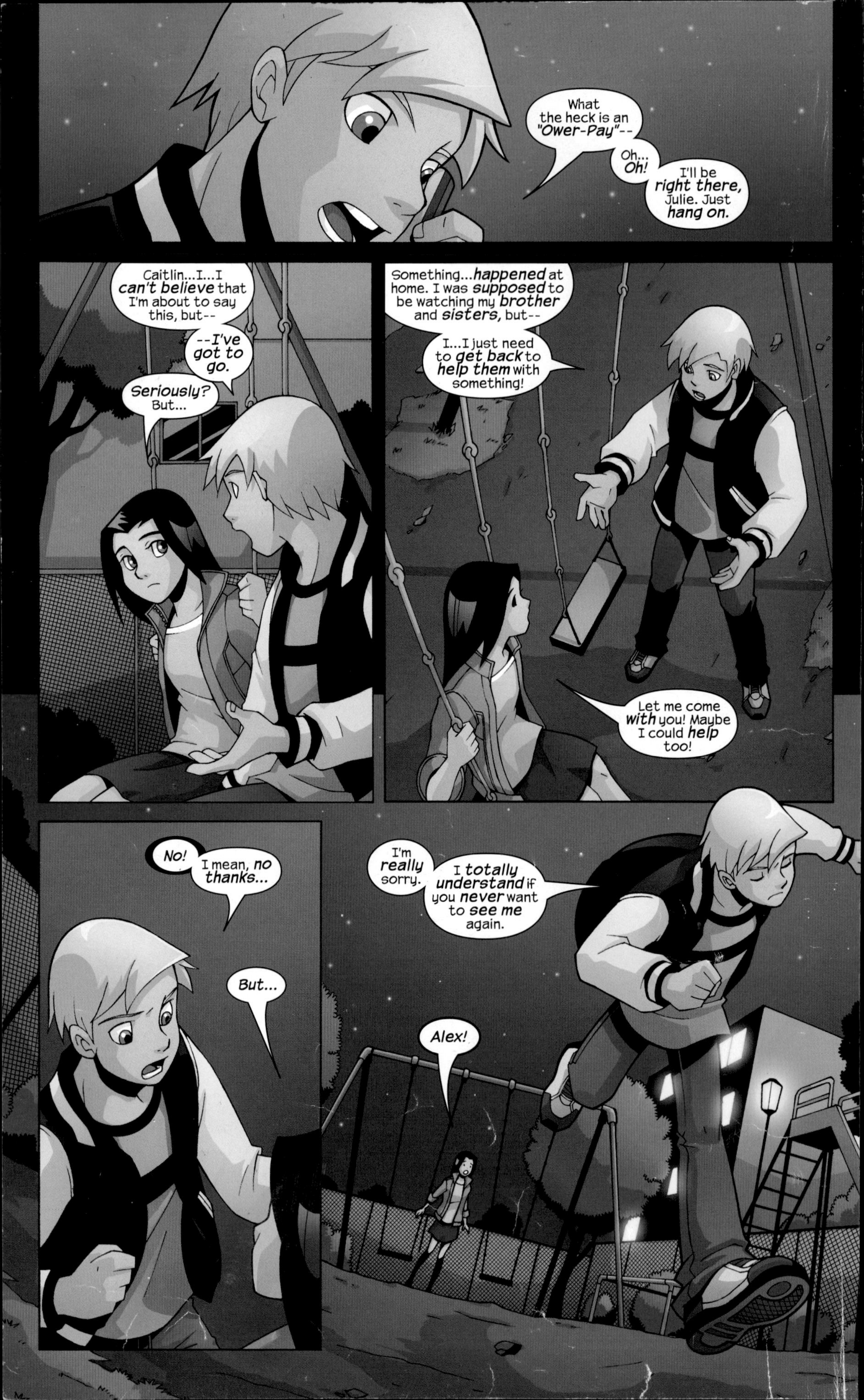
What the heck is an "Ower-Pay"--
Oh... Oh!
I'll be right there, Julie. Just hang on.
Caitlin...I...I can't believe that I'm about to say this, but--
--I've got to go.
Seriously? But...
Something...happened at home. I was supposed to be watching my brother and sisters, but--
I...I just need to get back to help them with something!
Let me come with you! Maybe I could help too!
No!
I mean, no thanks...
But...
I'm really sorry.
I totally understand if you never want to see me again.
Alex!

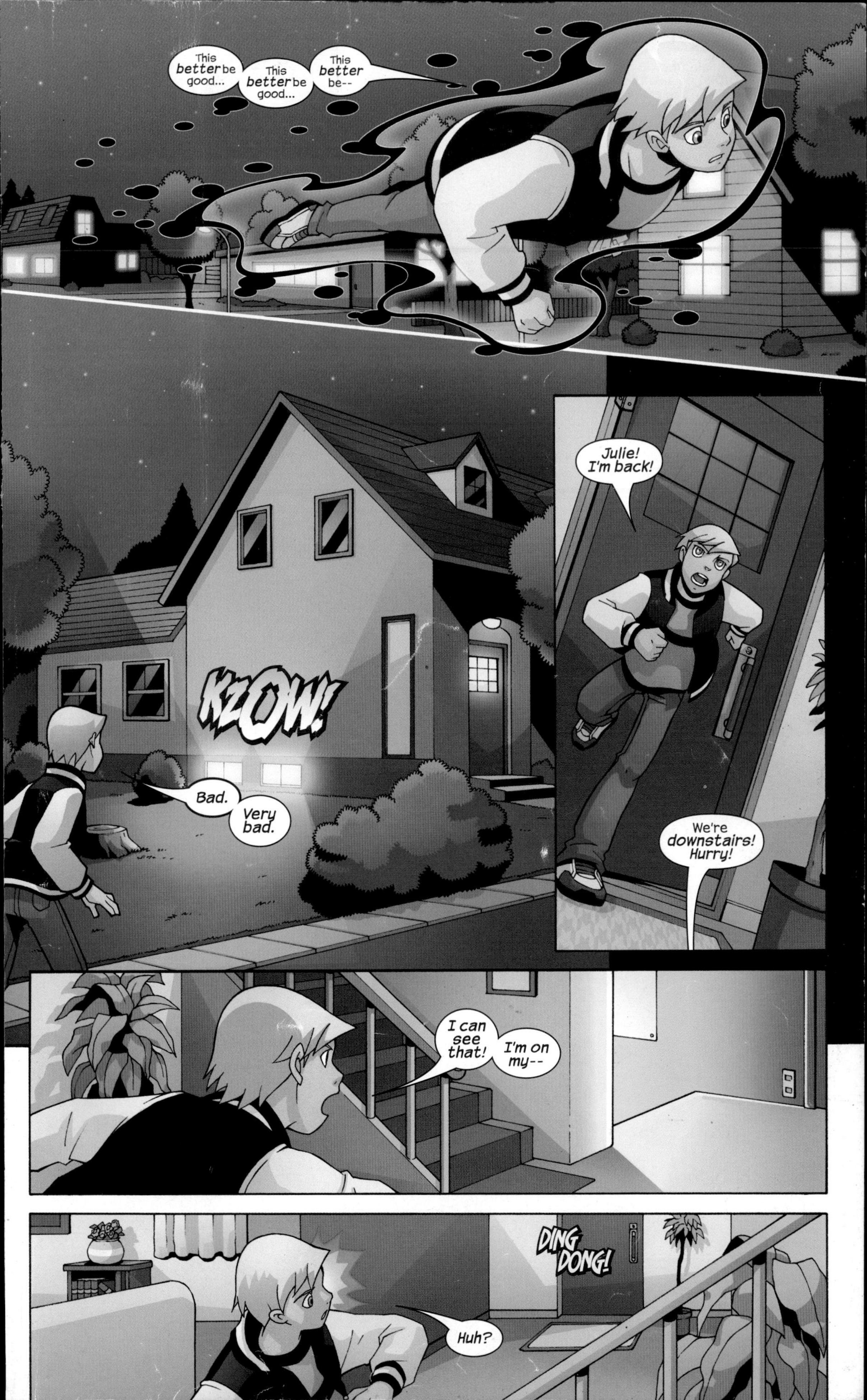

This better be good...
This better be good...
This better be--
KZOW!
Bad.
Very bad.
Julie! I'm back!
We're downstairs! Hurry!
I can see that!
I'm on my--
DING DONG!
Huh?

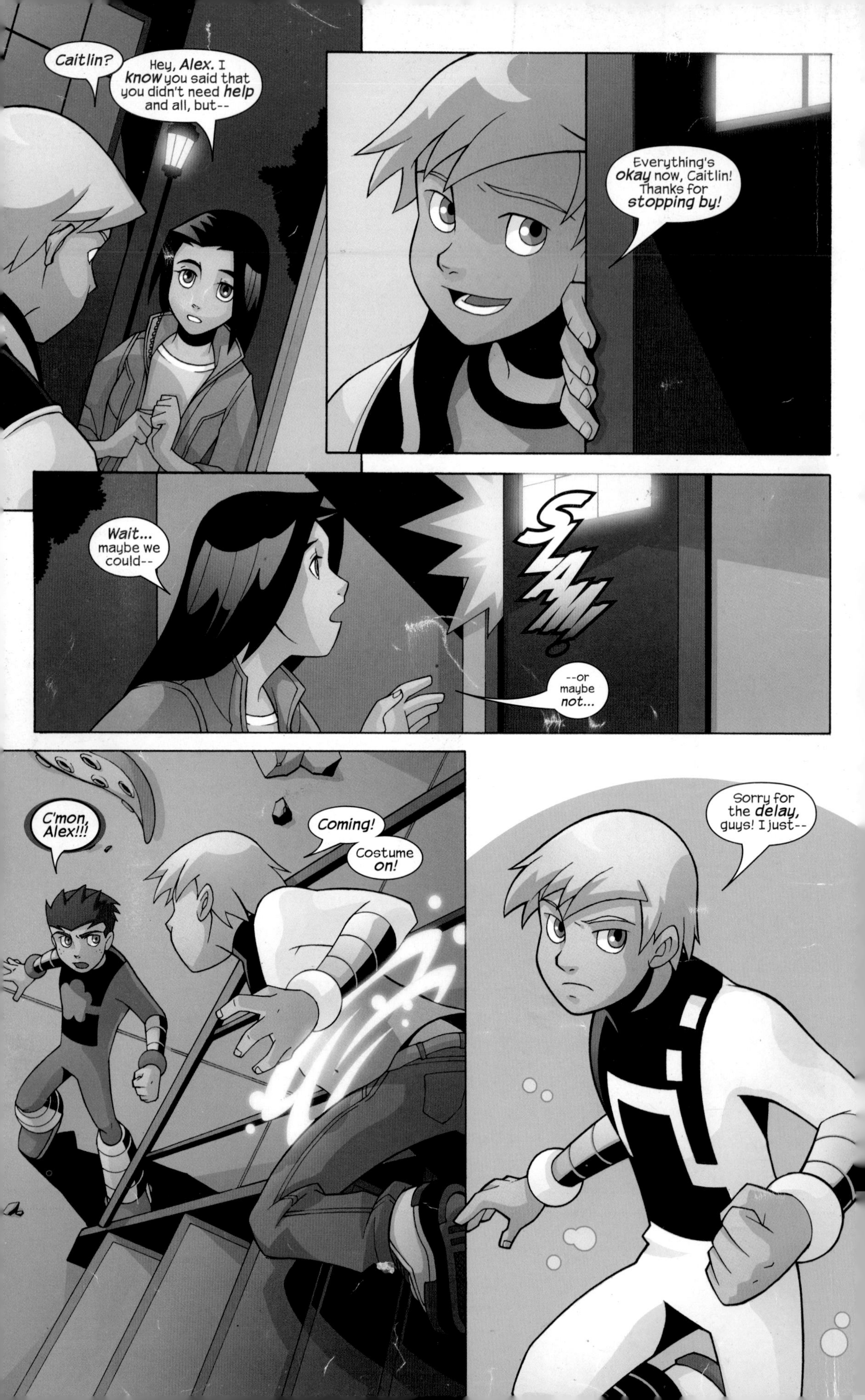
Caitlin?
Hey, Alex. I know you said that you didn't need help and all, but--
Everything's okay now, Caitlin! Thanks for stopping by!
Wait... maybe we could--
SLAM!
--or maybe not...
C'mon, Alex!!!
Coming!
Costume on!
Sorry for the delay, guys! I just--

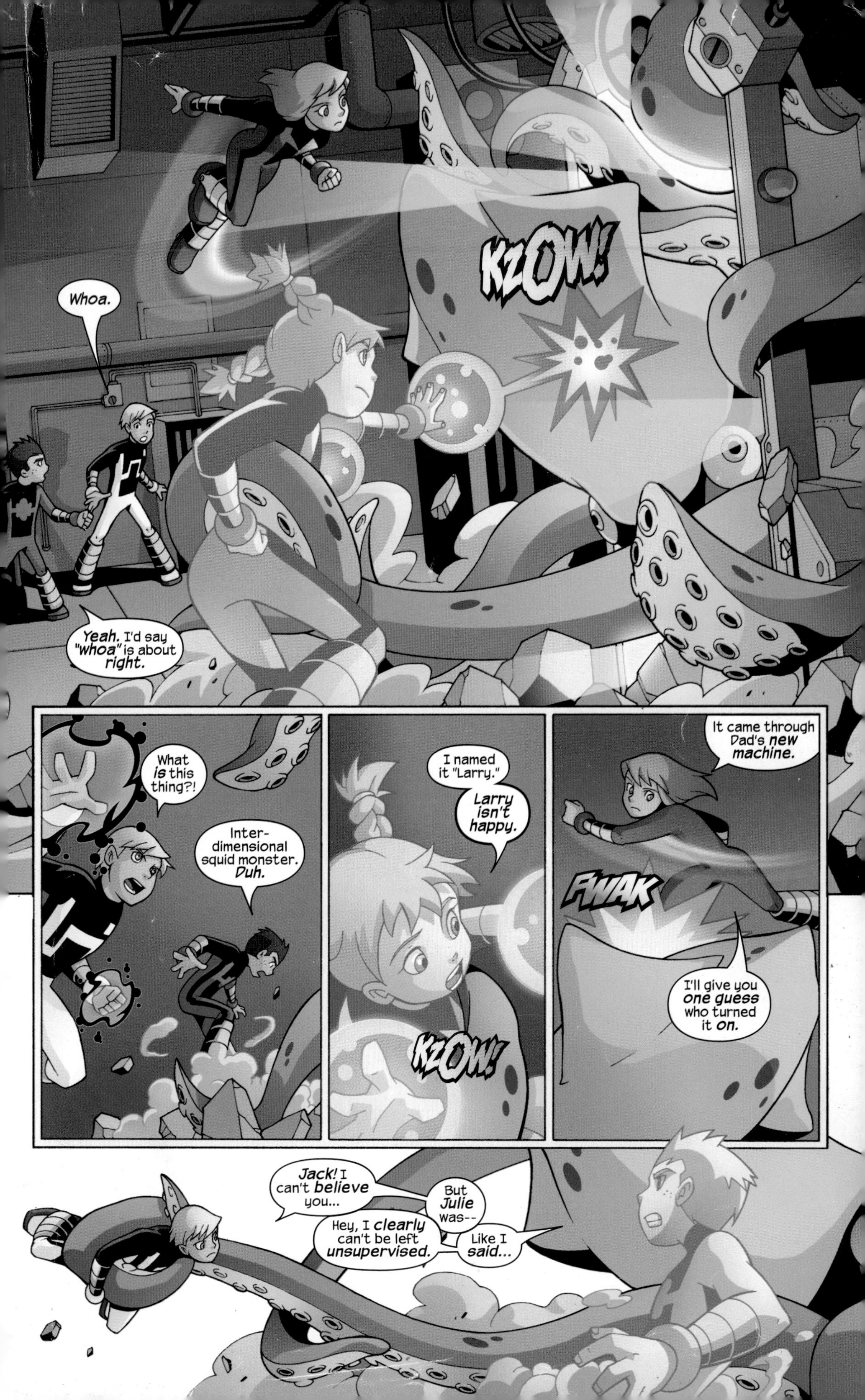

Whoa.
KZOW!
Yeah. I'd say "whoa" is about right.
What is this thing?!
Inter-dimensional squid monster. Duh.
I named it "Larry."
Larry isn't happy.
KZOW!
It came through Dad's new machine.
FWAK
I'll give you one guess who turned it on.
Jack! I can't believe you...
But Julie was--
Hey, I clearly can't be left unsupervised.
Like I said...

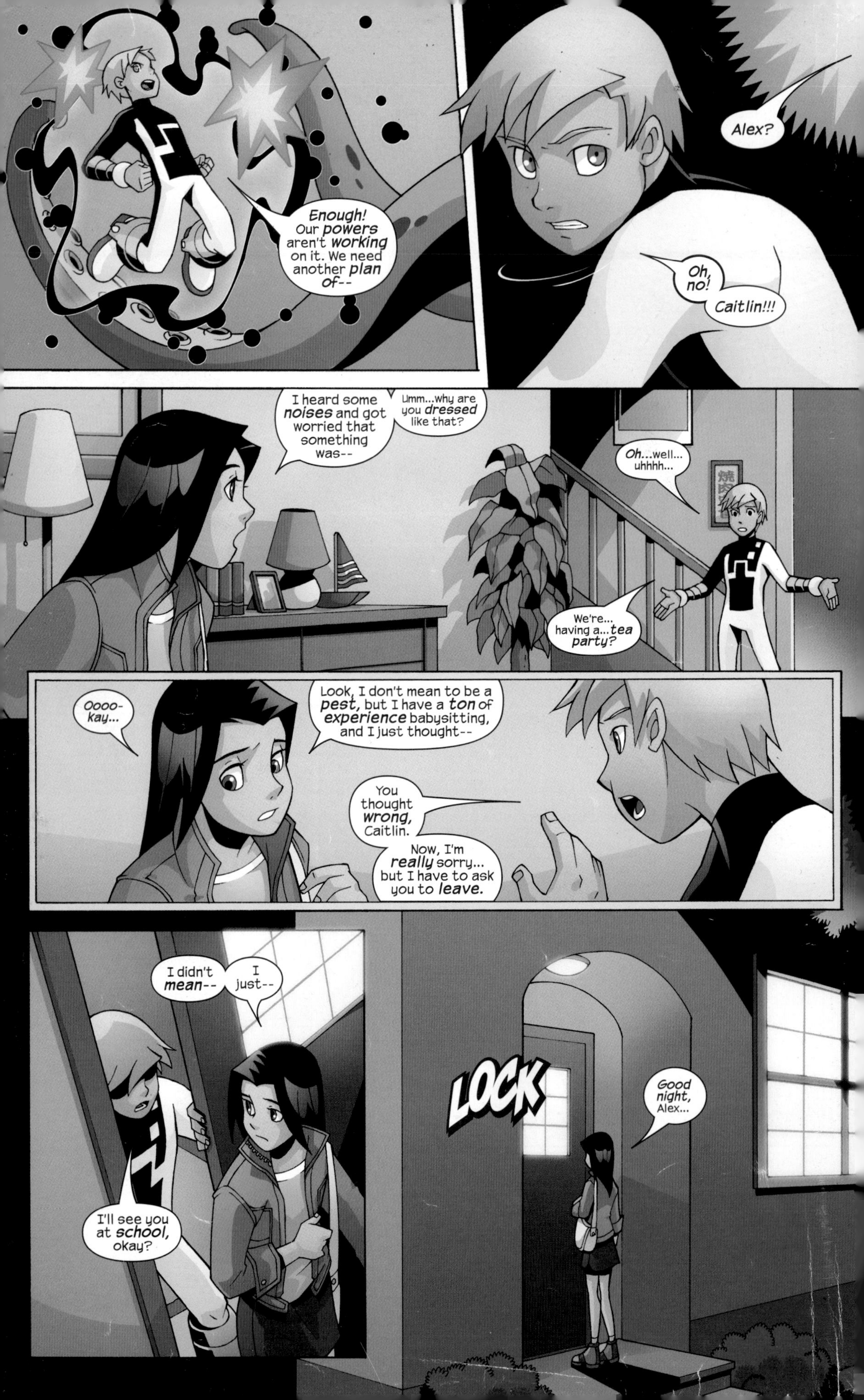
Enough! Our powers aren't working on it. We need another plan of--
Alex?
Oh, no!
Caitlin!!!
I heard some noises and got worried that something was--
Umm...why are you dressed like that?
Oh...well... uhhhh...
We're... having a...tea party?
Oooo-kay...
Look, I don't mean to be a pest, but I have a ton of experience babysitting, and I just thought--
You thought wrong, Caitlin.
Now, I'm really sorry... but I have to ask you to leave.
I didn't mean--
I just--
I'll see you at school, okay?
LOCK
Good night, Alex...

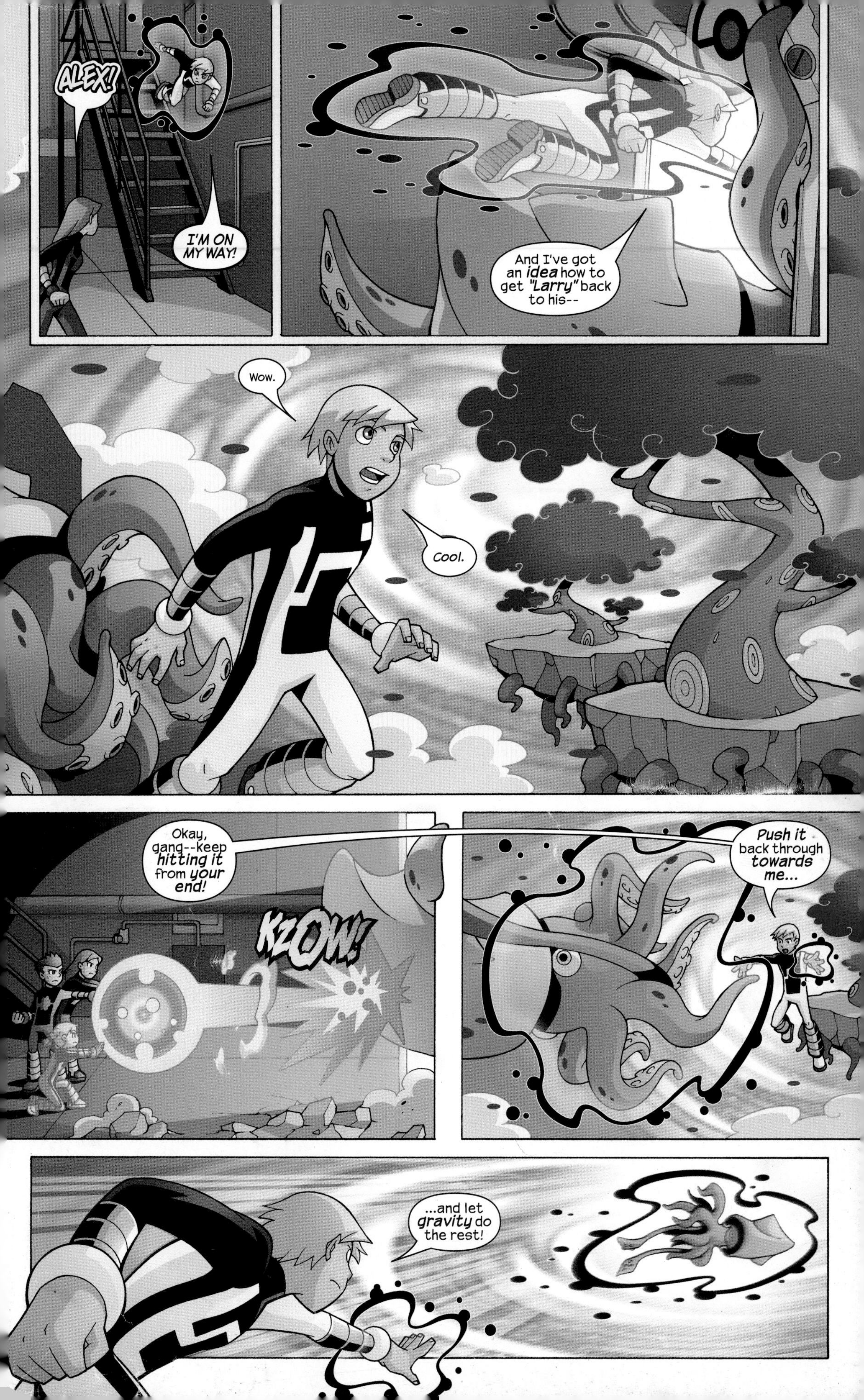
ALEX!
I'M ON MY WAY!
And I've got an *idea* how to get *"Larry"* back to his--
Wow.
Cool.
Okay, gang--keep *hitting it* from *your end!*
KZOW!
Push it back through *towards* me...
...and let *gravity* do the rest!

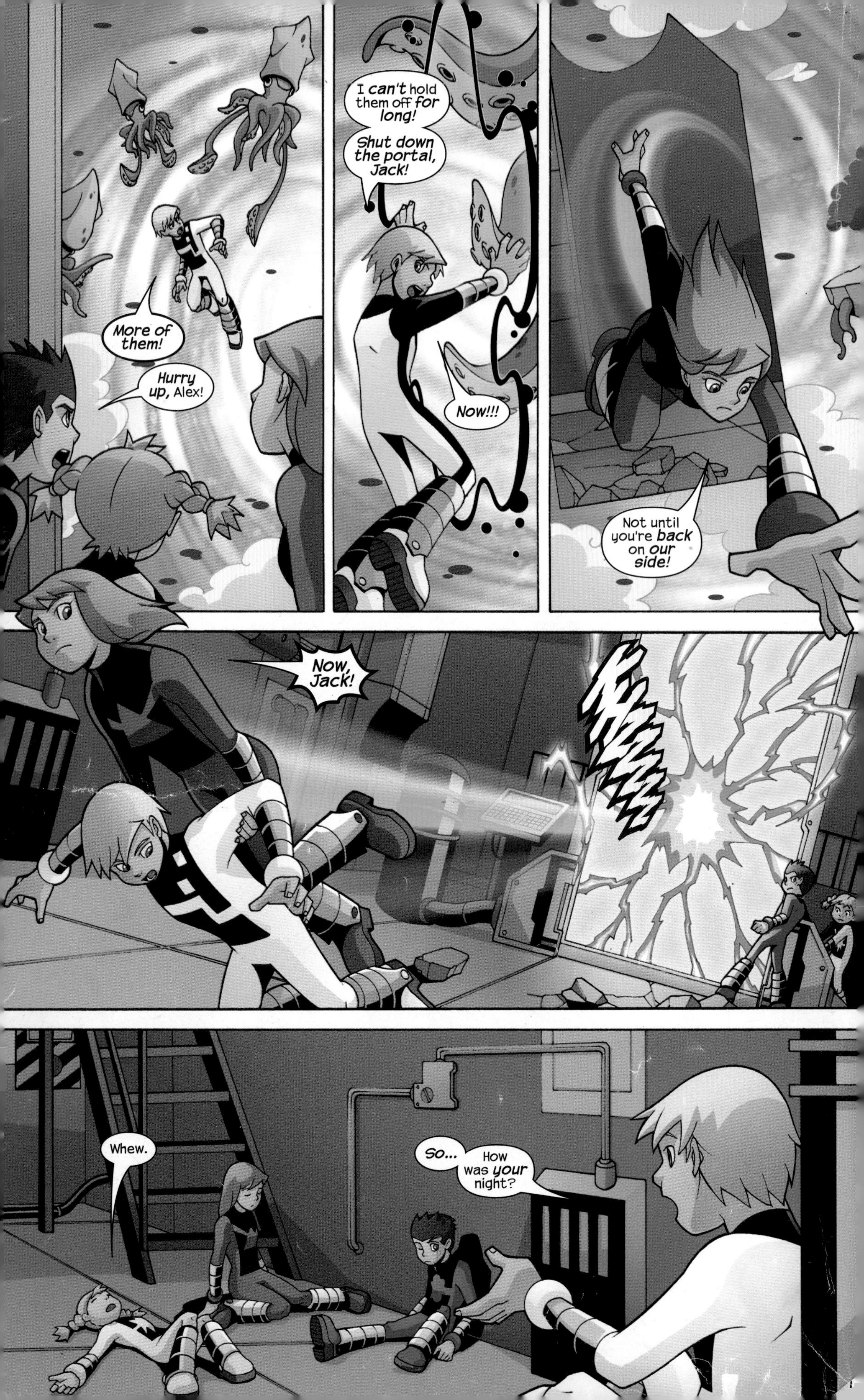
More of them!
Hurry up, Alex!
I can't hold them off for long!
Shut down the portal, Jack!
Now!!!
Not until you're back on our side!
Now, Jack!
Whew.
So... How was your night?

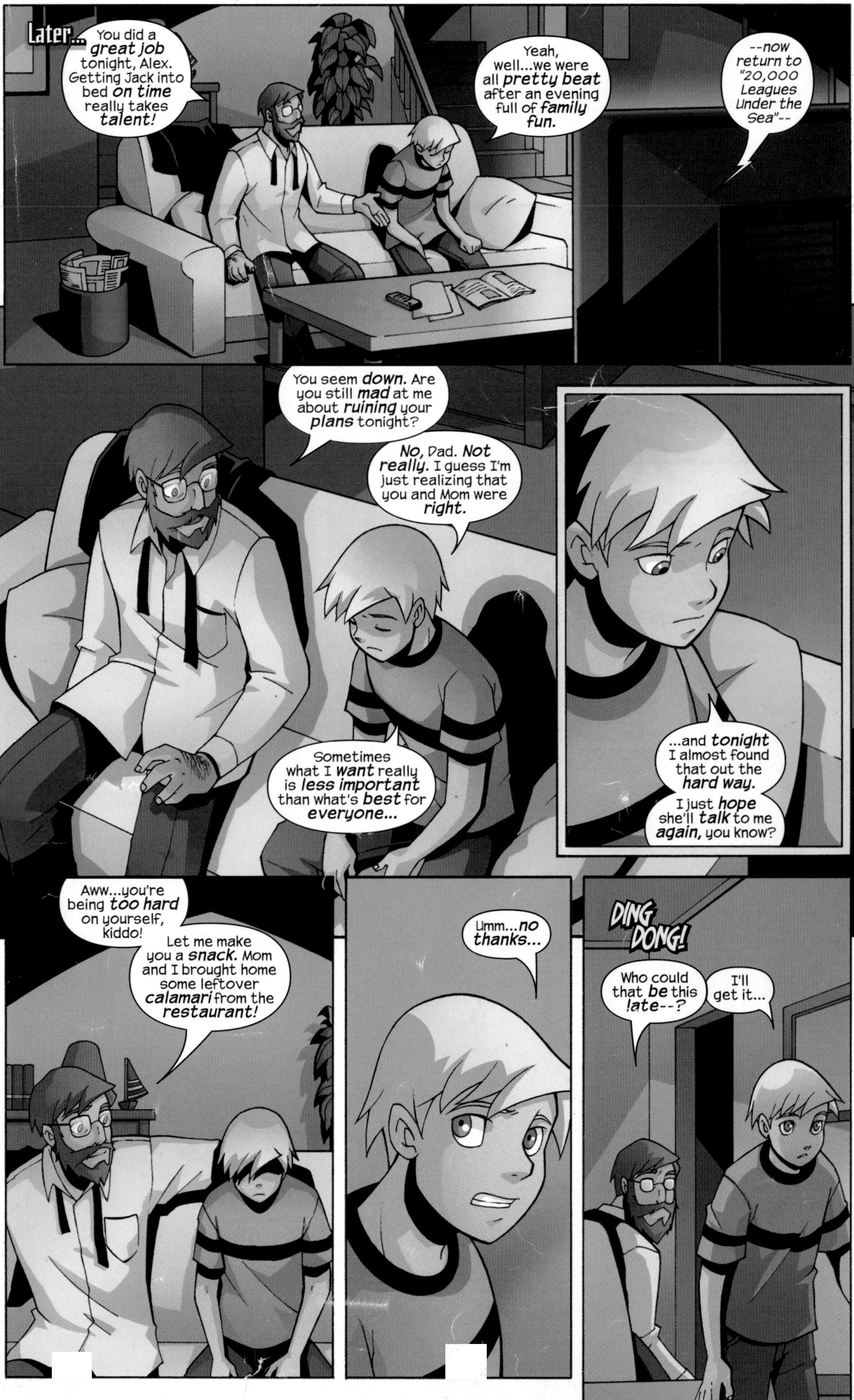
Later...
You did a great job tonight, Alex. Getting Jack into bed on time really takes talent!
Yeah, well...we were all pretty beat after an evening full of family fun.
--now return to "20,000 Leagues Under the Sea"--
You seem down. Are you still mad at me about ruining your plans tonight?
No, Dad. Not really. I guess I'm just realizing that you and Mom were right.
Sometimes what I want really is less important than what's best for everyone...
...and tonight I almost found that out the hard way.
I just hope she'll talk to me again, you know?
Aww...you're being too hard on yourself, kiddo!
Let me make you a snack. Mom and I brought home some leftover calamari from the restaurant!
Umm...no thanks...
DING DONG!
Who could that be this late--?
I'll get it...

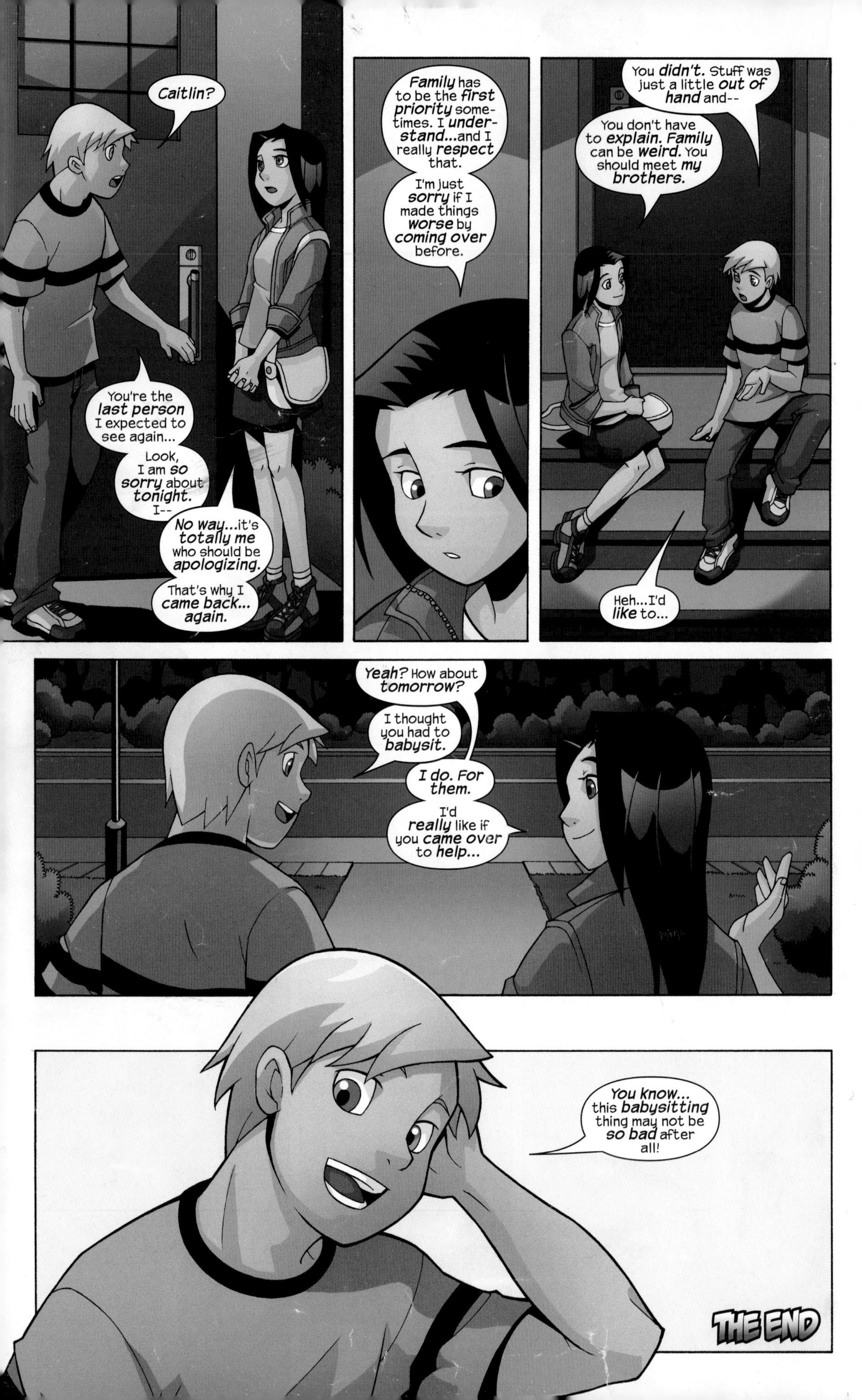
Caitlin?
You're the last person I expected to see again...
Look, I am so sorry about tonight. I--
No way...it's totally me who should be apologizing.
That's why I came back... again.
Family has to be the first priority sometimes. I understand...and I really respect that.
I'm just sorry if I made things worse by coming over before.
You didn't. Stuff was just a little out of hand and--
You don't have to explain. Family can be weird. You should meet my brothers.
Heh...I'd like to...
Yeah? How about tomorrow?
I thought you had to babysit.
I do. For them.
I'd really like if you came over to help...
You know... this babysitting thing may not be so bad after all!
THE END